For Kathy Henderson,
who had the idea

First published 1995 by
Walker Books Ltd
87 Vauxhall Walk, London SE11 5HJ

10 9 8 7 6 5 4 3 2 1

Text © year of publication
individual authors
Illustrations © year of publication
individual illustrators

Main cover illustration
© 1995 Helen Oxenbury

This book has been typeset
in Garamond.

Printed in Belgium

British Library Cataloguing
in Publication Data
A catalogue record for this book
is available from the British Library.

ISBN 0-7445-4407-6

WALKER BOOKS
AND SUBSIDIARIES
LONDON • BOSTON • SYDNEY

THE WALKER BABY BEAR

25 STORIES FOR THE VERY YOUNG

The Green Queen

The green queen lay in her

But she had to go out, so she got up

her black mac,  and her yellow

and orange and indigo scarf. And...

6

by Nick Sharratt

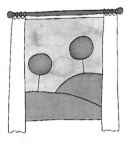

red bed and looked at the grey day.

She put on her blue shoes,

and pink and turquoise and brown

out she went.

7

When We Went to the Park
by Shirley Hughes

When Grandpa and I put on our coats and went to the park…

1  We saw one black cat sitting on a wall,

2  Two big girls licking ice-creams,

3

Three ladies chatting on a bench,

4

Four babies in buggies,

5  Five children playing in the sandpit,

6

Six runners running,

7

Seven dogs chasing one another,

8

Eight boys kicking a ball,

9

Nine ducks swimming on the pond,

10

Ten birds swooping in the sky, and so many leaves that I couldn't count them all.

On the way back we saw
the black cat again.
Then we went home for tea.

10

by Helen Oxenbury

Sometimes Pippo gets lost and I have to look for him. I asked Mummy if she'd seen Pippo, and she said I should look again in the toy-box. Pippo wasn't there, but I found his scarf.

Daddy said, "Have you looked under your bed?" But all I found there was Pippo's hat.

I got really worried
about Pippo and
thought I might
never see him again.

Mummy said Pippo couldn't be far away
and we should look in the sitting room.

And that's where he'd been all the time, in the bookcase.

If Pippo is going off on his own, I've told him he really should let me know.

Let's

Can you find your ears?

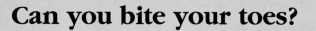

Can you bite your toes?

Can you find your eyes?

by Amy MacDonald

14

Do It

Can you play peek-a-boo?

Can you touch your nose?

Can you wave bye-bye?

illustrated by Maureen Roffey

Where's My Mummy?

by Colin and Jacqui Hawkins

17

MOTHER GOOSE

LITTLE BOY BLUE

Little Boy Blue,
 Come blow your horn,
The sheep's in the meadow,
 The cow's in the corn;
But where is the boy
 Who looks after the sheep?
He's under a haycock,
 Fast asleep.
Will you wake him?
 No, not I,
For if I do,
 He's sure to cry.

18

Three poems illustrated by
Michael Foreman

TO THE MAGPIE
Magpie, magpie, flutter and flee,
Turn up your tail and good luck come to me.

BAA, BAA, BLACK SHEEP
Baa, baa, black sheep,
    Have you any wool?
Yes sir, yes sir,
    Three bags full:
One for the master,
    And one for the dame,
And one for the little boy
    Who lives down the lane.

Here Come the Babies

What does a baby do?

jumble

juggle

jump

bang

burp

bump

totter

tumble

throw

gurgle

giggle

grow

by Catherine and Laurence Anholt

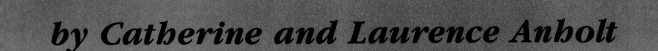

What are babies like?

Babies kick
and babies crawl,

Slide their potties down the hall.

Babies smile
and babies yell,

This one has
a funny smell.

fish

horse

lizard

parrot

guinea pig

COW

animals by Lucy Cousins

donkey

duck

hen

pig

rabbit

cat

goose

cock

A You're Adorable

A you're a‑dor‑a‑ble, B you're so beau‑ti‑ful, C you're a cu‑tie full of charms,

D you're a dar‑ling and E you're ex‑cit‑ing and F you're a feath‑er in my arms.

G you look good to me, H you're so hea‑ven‑ly, I you're the one I i‑dol‑ize,

J we're like Jack and Jill, K you're so kiss‑a‑ble, L is the love‑light in your eyes.

A song by Buddy Kaye, Fred Wise and Sidney Lippman

M, N, O, P, I could go on — all day. Q, R,

S, T, al-pha-bet-i-cally speak-ing you're O-K! — U made my life com-plete,

V means you're ver-y sweet, W——— X, Y, Z— It's

fun to wan-der through the al-pha-bet with you to tell you what you mean to me!—

illustrated by Martha Alexander

OLD MOTHER HUBBARD

**Old Mother Hubbard
Went to the cupboard,**

To fetch her poor dog a bone;
But when she got there
The cupboard was bare
And so the poor dog had none.

She went to the baker's
To buy him some bread;
But when she came back
The poor dog was dead.

She went to the fishmonger's
To buy him some fish;
But when she came back
He was licking the dish.

She went to the undertaker's
To buy him a coffin;
But when she came back
The poor dog was laughing.

She took a clean dish
To get him some tripe;
But when she came back
He was smoking a pipe.

She went to the hatter's
To buy him a hat;
But when she came back
He was feeding the cat.

illustrated by Elizabeth Wood

She went to the tailor's
To buy him a coat;
But when she came back
He was riding a goat.

She went to the cobbler's
To buy him some shoes;
But when she came back
He was reading the news.

She went to the seamstress
To buy him some linen;
But when she came back
The dog was a-spinning.

She went to the barber's
To buy him a wig;
But when she came back
He was dancing a jig.

She went to the hosier's
To buy him some hose;
But when she came back
He was dressed in his clothes.

The dame made a curtsey,
The dog made a bow;
The dame said, *"Your servant,"*
The dog said, *"Bow-wow."*

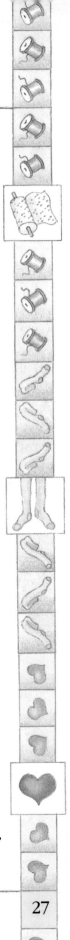

I Love Animals

by Flora McDonnell

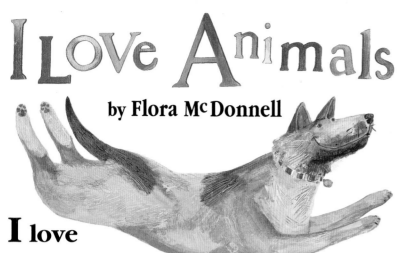

I love
Jock, my dog.

I love the ducks
waddling to the water.

I love
the donkey
braying
"hee-haw!"

I love
the pony
rolling
over and
over.

I love the turkey
strutting round
the yard.

I love
the hens
hopping up
and down.

I love the pig with all
her little piglets.

I love
the cow
swishing
her tail.

I love
the goat
racing across
the field.

I love the sheep bleating
to her lamb.

I love
all the
animals.

I hope
they love
me.

Sleeping

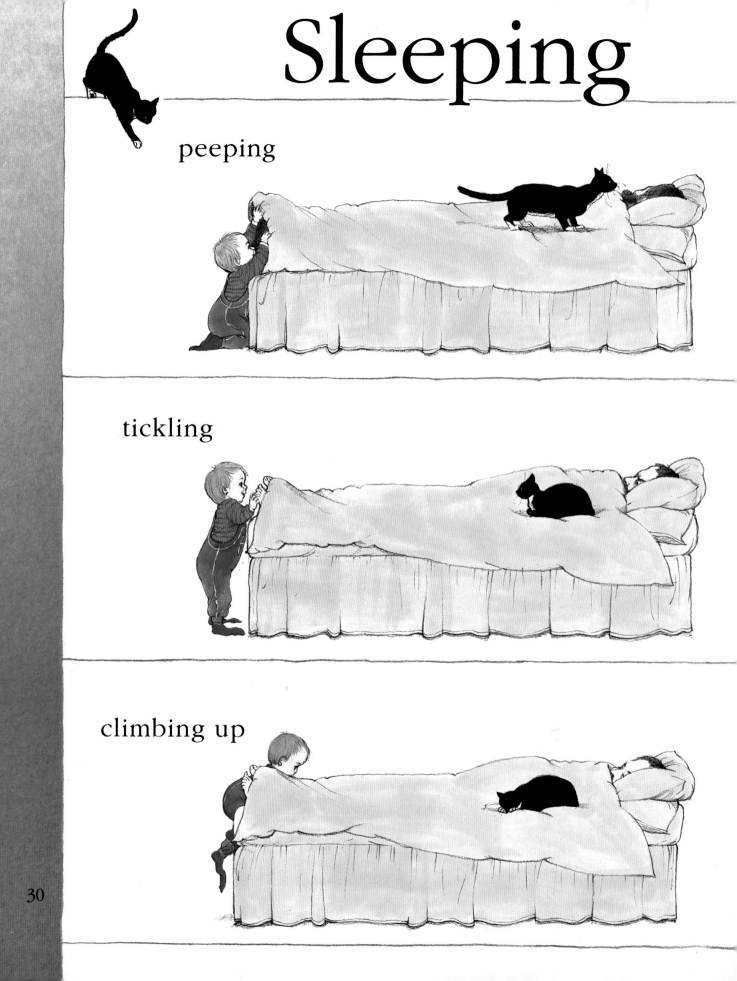

peeping

tickling

climbing up

by Jan Ormerod

bouncing

pulling his nose

cuddling

31

HUMPTY DUMPTY

illustrated by Julie Lacome

Humpty Dumpty
Sat on a wall,
Humpty Dumpty
Had a great fall.

All the king's horses
And all the king's men
Couldn't put Humpty
Together again.

My Cat Jack

by Patricia Casey

My cat Jack is a yawning cat.
He's a stretching-down cat. He's a stretching-up cat.

My cat Jack is a scratching cat.
He's a curling cat. He's a lapping cat.

My cat Jack is a purring cat,
a rough-tongued cat, a washing cat.

He's a cat who likes washing all over.

My cat Jack is a playing cat.
He's a pouncing cat. He's an acrobat cat.

And sometimes he's a silly old cat.
I love him, my cat Jack.

Clara Vulliamy # Blue Hat

orange gloves

blue hat

red coat

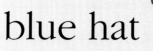

brown jumper

Red Coat

 green socks

black shoes

purple trousers

pink T-shirt

 yellow vest

white nappy

... all gone!

Animals

by Helen Oxenbury

Jill the Farmer
and her friends

by Nick Butterworth

Pete is a mechanic.

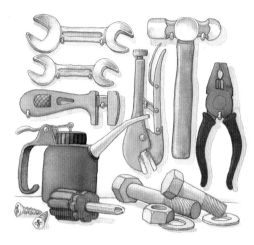

What does he use?

Betty is a baker.

What does she sell?

40

Fred is a dustman.

What does he collect?

Anna is a doctor.

Why has she come?

Jim is a messenger.

What does he ride?

Grey plane

CHARLOTTE VOAKE'S

COLOURS

PURPLE

RED

Brown
trailer

Green tractor

Red
truck

42

Blue train

ORANGE

Black

BLUE

YELLOW

PINK

BROWN

GREEN

Yellow boat

Pink car

Black bike

Four black puppies in a basket, fast asleep.

One black puppy
waking up.

One black puppy
going for a walk.

44

PUPPIES

by
Sally Grindley   illustrated by
Clive Scruton

One black puppy
pulling at an apron.

One shopping basket
falling down.

CRASH!

Three black puppies running in to have a look.

Three black puppies
see ... A GHOST!

One white puppy chasing
three black puppies.

All four puppies running
round and round.

All four puppies
running back to bed.

All four puppies in a basket, fast asleep.

cluck baa

hiss

cluck

hoot

croak

neigh

48

by John Burningham

quack

moo

roar

buzz

baa

49

Noah's Ark

A long time ago there lived a man called Noah.

Noah was a good man, who trusted in God.

There were also many wicked people in the world.

God wanted to punish the wicked people,

so he said to Noah…

I shall make a flood of water and wash all the wicked people away. Build an ark for your family and all the animals.

Noah worked for years and years and years to build the ark.

At last the ark was finished.

Noah and his family gathered lots of food.

Then the animals came, two by two, two by two, into the ark.

retold and illustrated by Lucy Cousins

When the ark was full Noah felt a drop of rain. It rained
and rained and rained. It rained for forty days
and forty nights. The world was covered with water.
At last the rain stopped and the sun
came out. Noah sent a dove to find
dry land. The dove came
back with a leafy twig.
"Hurrah!" shouted Noah.
"The flood has ended."
But many more days passed
before the ark came to rest
on dry land.
Then Noah and all the animals
came safely out of the ark,
and life began
again on
the earth.

Bumpety Bump

A Knee-ride Rhyme

by Kathy Henderson *illustrated by Carol Thompson*

The baby went for a ride,
***a-bumpety-
bumpety-bump!***

She rode in her sister's arms,
***a-slumpety-
slumpety-slump!***

She rode on her
grandpa's knee,
***a-tumpety-
tumpety-tump!***

She rode on her mother's hip,
***a-lumpety-
lumpety-lump!***

She rode on her uncle's neck,
***a-humpety-
humpety-hump!***

And flew high up in the air,
***a-jumpety-
jumpety-jump!***

She rode around and
about and then …
went back to sleep
in her cot again.

Things I Like

by Anthony Browne

*This is me
and this is
what I like:*

Painting …
and riding my bike.

Playing with toys,
and dressing up.

Making a cake …
and watching TV.

Going to birthday
parties, and being
with my friends.

Having a bath …
hearing a
bedtime story …

Climbing trees …
and kicking a ball.

Hiding …
and acrobatics.

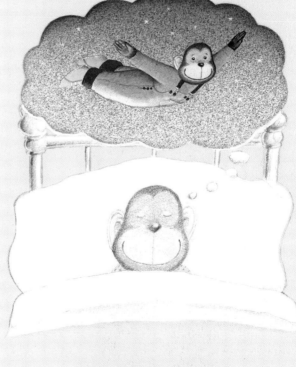

and dreaming.

Where's Billy?

You hide, Billy.
I'll find you.

What a funny bag!
It has feet.

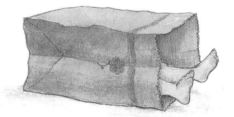

That bag
walks.

by *Martha Alexander*

It's following me.
It's running!

The bag's fallen down.

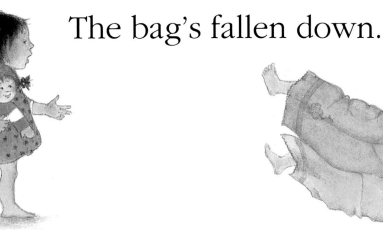

It's Billy!
I've found you!

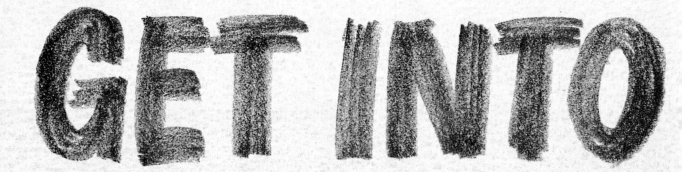

GET INTO

It was time for Bartholomew to go to bed.

"Ba, time for bed,"
George said.

"Nah!" said
Bartholomew.

Nah

George said, "Brush your
teeth and go to bed."
"Nah!" said Bartholomew.

58

BED!

by
Virginia Miller

"Have you brushed
your teeth yet, Ba?"
"Nah!" said Bartholomew,
beginning to cry.

"Come on, Ba, into bed!"
George said.
"Nah!" said Bartholomew.
"Nah, nah, nah, nah,
NAH!" said Bartholomew.

"Get into bed!"

George said in a big voice.
Bartholomew got into bed.

He giggled and wriggled, he hid and tiggled,

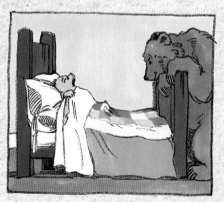

he cuddled and huggled, he snuggled and sighed.

"Goodnight, Bartholomew," said George.
"Nah," said Bartholomew softly.
He gave a big yawn, closed his eyes
and went to sleep.